Exiled!

Wildfire was immediately alerted by the call. It seemed to him that Whinny was threatening his authority; this time, the colt had gone too far. He charged after the colt and pushed against him so hard that Whinny nearly fell over.

Whinny tore off toward the hills. The stallion kept chasing him until he crossed the stream.

No longer hearing the pounding of hoofs behind him, Whinny slowed down. He looked back. Wildfire was still watching him. Whinny knew he couldn't go back.

Whinny
of the
Wild Horses

by AMY C. LAUNDRIE

Illustrated by Jean Cassels Helmer

BULLSEYE BOOKS · ALFRED A. KNOPF
NEW YORK

My thanks to some special friends,
Susan Casper and Daniel Dieterich,
who believed I had a story to tell
—A. C. L.

PART I

With one last push from the mare, the foal slipped out of his mother's body. He took a gulp of air, then breathed steadily. The cold, damp ground was an uncomfortable surprise, and he bleated loudly in protest.

The mare bent down to nuzzle him, then licked him vigorously until he was warm and clean. He slowly opened his eyes and saw a dark shadow against the early morning light.

Shadow continued licking her son, her tongue moving over his short mane. While Shadow was a rich chocolate color, the foal was the same satiny reddish chestnut as his sire. The arch of his tail and neck showed that he had some Arabian blood. His body was sturdy and muscular. Alert brown eyes, hedged by long lashes, looked up at her with curiosity, as if the little colt were already planning some mischief.

Shadow gave a great cry of pleasure. "Whin-nee-ee-ey!" she called. Upon hearing his new name, Whinny flapped his tail on the ground. Then, because he liked the thumping sound it made, he flapped it again.

After all this excitement, Whinny felt the need for something. He wasn't sure exactly what it was, but he knew his mother was the one who could help. To get closer to her, he would have to raise himself up.

Whinny's legs were very long and skinny; they were tucked up under his body. He tried to unfold them, staring at the knobby knees. Spreading them wide, he lifted himself up. Whinny wavered a bit but remained standing. Amazed at his accomplishment, he boldly tried a step. But his long legs suddenly tangled around each other, and he collapsed in a heap.

The mare nuzzled him, urging him to try again. Shadow knew there were wolves in the area, and she was anxious to return to the safety of the band. Whinny sensed his mother's urgency and tried again. This time he raised himself, allowed himself the time to balance on all four legs, then cautiously swung one foot wide. He had taken his first step.

He gingerly took another step; now he was underneath the mare. He nuzzled her, first her legs, then her shoulders, then her belly. He pushed here and there, delighted finally to discover the warm, sweet milk she had waiting for him. Shadow turned her head and gave a little nickering sound. Whinny sucked noisily, flapping his fuzzy tail with excitement. He drank until his sides bulged; then he took a nap.

Shadow gazed off across the Wyoming range to the valley far below, searching for signs of danger. Then she raised her head to test the air for any predators' scent. This was wilderness country, with hills and peaks surrounding valleys and plains. Yesterday, while her band of wild mustangs was grazing in the valley, Shadow had started off on her own. She had climbed to this sheltered plateau because she had wanted to give birth in privacy.

Whinny woke and sniffed the air, too; he smelled new grass and earth damp from the spring rains. Shadow took several steps, then called to her son. Cautiously at first, Whinny wobbled alongside. His steps became steadier, and soon he was trotting. Shadow headed straight for the place the band had last been, the south end of Wild Horse Valley.

They traveled for several hours before she realized the band must have moved elsewhere. Twilight fell. Mare and foal found a sheltered place to spend the night. Snuggled against each other for warmth, they heard the far-off howl of a wolf summoning the pack for a hunt. Shadow grew nervous, and her nostrils flared when the howl was answered by another wolf.

She rested fitfully that night. Whinny woke at dawn and found his mother's dark milk bag im-

mediately. He nursed deeply. His movements were much more confident today, and he was stronger. He followed the mare closely when Shadow began to head for the north end of the valley, the band's summer home.

They came to a patch of tender grass, and Shadow paused to graze. Whinny's ears flicked forward as

he watched two magpies flit from rock to rock. He explored a little further, sniffing at a bunch of violets. Shadow sniffed, too, but when she caught the scent of wolves, her nostrils flared in alarm. Her ears tilted forward to catch every sound. She stamped her foot fretfully and called to her youngster. Hearing the terror in his mother's voice, Whinny dashed back to her.

They traveled north at a fast pace. It was midday, with still no sign of the other horses, when Whinny stepped into a badger hole. His knees buckled, sending him sprawling on the ground. The mare nickered to him to hurry and get up, but he couldn't. Then she gave him a warning nip. Shadow didn't want to be left without the band's protection another night.

"*Whin-nee-ee-ey!*" the colt cried in protest. His mother nudged him frantically, afraid now that Whinny was hurt. A broken leg would be sure death in wolf country.

Whinny struggled to stand. Then he took a few steps. His legs were not broken, only shaky from weariness.

The two horses began traveling steadily once again. As the sun sank lower in the sky, they came to the northern end of the valley. Shadow recognized the scent of her band at last, and she whickered with excitement. Her little foal was safe.

CHAPTER 2

Through the lush grass of the valley flowed a swiftly running brook. Forget-me-nots, with their miniature blue flowers, grew in abundance along its shore. Aspen and cottonwood trees thrived in the moist soil. Upland, thrushes and bluebirds added sweet song to the countryside. The meadow was surrounded by slopes and high ridges, which gave way to even steeper cliffs off in the distance. With these as a barrier, Wild Horse Valley was a protected little world within the vast range.

Whinny caught sight of something moving swiftly toward them. It was big, bigger even than his mother, and it shimmered as it headed straight for them. Suddenly it stopped. They had found the leader of the band.

Wildfire stood alert, his thickly muscled legs quivering, his sides heaving in and out from the run. His proud head was flung back, his red-gold tail and mane blowing in the wind. The stallion blew softly against Shadow's neck. This was his lead mare, who helped him keep the band in line. Happy to have her back, he caressed her, touching her soft muzzle, then began to sniff her.

Whinny felt a new emotion, jealousy, as Wildfire continued to nuzzle and study Shadow. Finally, when he was satisfied she was all right, the stallion turned to Whinny. He nickered a greeting; Whinny noticed that his voice was deeper and brassier than Shadow's. Then Wildfire inspected his son's sturdy body. His sire's scrutiny made Whinny uncomfortable, and he was glad when Wildfire started to lead them down the slope to meet the other horses.

A group of sixteen horses was grazing in a wide meadow along the stream. There were horses of various sizes and colors: mares, foals, and one gelding; bays and blacks, solids and pintos. Whinny was a late colt; the other mares had already given birth that spring. Of the nine foals born, a mountain lion, wolves, and a late-winter storm had reduced the number to six. One foal was an Appaloosa; another was a pale honey color. There was a reddish brown bay filly with a black mane and tail, and another filly that was totally black. There were two foals that resembled Wildfire—Whinny and a delicate filly, Starfire. Her red-gold coat made a striking contrast against her creamy-colored mane and tail.

Starfire was nursing from her mother. She paused and looked at Whinny with interest. The mare—

Goldie, a golden palomino—bore the brand of a nearby ranch. At first when Wildfire had tried to steal her away, Goldie had refused to go. But after several bites on the rump, she had finally relented. Goldie occasionally missed her warm barn and bag of oats, but she knew she belonged with the band now.

Standing apart from the mares was Ol' Dan, a gelding who had also been part of a ranch. His owners had turned him loose when they no longer could use him. Wildfire had let him join the band, knowing he was no threat to his leadership.

Shadow was immediately met by a chocolate-colored filly with a thick mane—a miniature Shadow. This was Whinny's sister, Filly. The little yearling raised her head sharply and studied him. Then she greeted her mother, nuzzling up to her, but Shadow pushed her away. Again Filly tried, but this time big yellow teeth nipped her in the neck.

Filly walked away, hanging her head. She had seen other mares reject their yearlings when they had a new foal, and she had seen the stallion drive them away. Forcing them to leave the band was nature's way of preventing inbreeding, but Filly didn't understand that. She met up with another yearling, and together they walked to the stream. Whinny came to Shadow then and nursed.

In the next several days, Shadow rested and ate the sweet timothy and redtop grass, and the rich clover that grew by the stream. The air was filled with the perfume of sun-warmed earth and wild strawberries.

Summer began. Filly came back several times, but Shadow always chased her away. Finally, Wildfire took off after her, and the yearling left for good. Whinny watched as she ran along the stream. The time had come for Filly to find a herd of her own.

Summer was a time of plenty, a time to grow, and a time of discovery. The mares munched lazily and drank from the steam. The foals nursed, played, slept, then played some more. Whinny began to eat grass; it was bitter, tasting nothing like his mother's sweet milk, but it filled him up between nursings. He grew familiar with the other animals that came to the stream.

The young colt's curiosity got him into trouble more than once. His mother taught him to be alert for the scent of mountain lions, coyotes, and wolves, but she had never warned him about smaller animals.

One day Whinny came upon a newly born antelope that lay hidden in the grass. At this age, the fawn had little scent, and Whinny almost blundered right into it. He stared at the fawn's tan-and-white face, the ears that lay plastered against its neck, and the slender legs tucked under its body.

Whinny sniffed at the little creature, and when it didn't move, he licked it curiously. The fawn whined, then growled. Suddenly, Whinny heard twigs breaking. He turned to see the fawn's mother coming straight for him. The pronghorn's head was lowered. She stamped her sharp hoofs and snorted in warning. Whinny quickly galloped away to find his mother.

Not long after, Whinny met another curious-looking animal. It proved to be an unlucky day when he noticed a pretty white-and-black-striped animal waddling along the stream, followed by her five kits. Whinny trotted over to investigate, greatly taken with their fluffy tails and their strong odor. But when he tried to get better acquainted, the mother thumped the ground with her paws in warning.

When Whinny continued to approach, the skunk mother swiveled her hips, swung her fluffy tail aside, and sent a stream of spray directly at the young horse. Her aim was true. Whinny felt the spray sting his eyes and settle into his coat. He snorted, wheezed, and coughed, trying to rid himself of the musky odor. But it was no use. Once again he ran home to his mother—but this time Shadow wasn't quite as anxious to comfort him. In fact, before he had even met her, she started cantering away. Whinny was beginning to learn the consequences of being too curious.

Rainfall was sparse in the valley that summer, and the deep blue sky showed little promise of any rain to come. The grass began to turn brown from lack of water. The horses took dust baths, rolling

on the ground to rid themselves of the dirt and sweat that was caked on their coats.

Wildfire, as tender of the band, was on constant guard against danger. One evening while the horses were settling down for the night, Wildfire made his final wide circle around them. He had just finished, and was about to go to the stream for a drink, when his ears twitched. He could hear horses and feel the vibration of their approach. His nostrils flared as he tested for their scent. His red muzzle lifted and quivered, his eyes staring off at the horizon.

Then he saw them: four riders with two packhorses. Wildfire pawed the ground, then reared up on his back legs. The riders stopped abruptly, dismounted, and began talking in low voices.

One gave a whistle. "My, but he's a beauty. And that's some harem he has. Wouldn't mind capturing him for myself."

Stan Preston, the leader of the group, shook his head. "Larry, you just better remember what you're hired to do. If I don't get rid of every last one of these horses, there ain't going to be enough range left for my new cattle. Now, we'd best make camp. We have to get an early start in the morning. And don't be making a lot of noise, or you'll spook the herd."

While Preston and Larry unloaded the packhorses, the other two cattlemen started a fire. Wildfire watched them uneasily, keeping on the alert. He allowed the band to graze and to go to the stream for water, but he wouldn't let them wander.

The men had shot two jack rabbits and a sage hen on the way. It wasn't long before the hungry men had the game roasting on a spit over the fire, two cans of beans warming in the flames, and potatoes baking around the edge. After the men had filled their plates, they sat around the fire and began to eat. When their plates were empty and the coffee was ready, they settled down to talk.

"So," began an older cowhand by the name of Jake, "what's the plan for tomorrow?"

Preston, who liked to talk with his hands, was forced to put down his coffee. "Gentlemen," he said, "the plan is simple. We drive the mustangs out of the valley to the ridge, and from there we head them toward the cliffs."

"Why not just shoot 'em and be done with it?" Larry asked, letting a stream of tobacco juice fly so it sizzled on the fire.

"Makes too much noise. Driving 'em off a cliff is quieter, and the evidence is sure harder to go after."

Jake rose to put another log on the campfire. "What do you need more cattle for anyway, Boss? Seems to me you got plenty already."

Preston laughed. "I aim to make me enough on this herd to get an even bigger spread. The only thing standing between me and half of Wyoming is one lousy herd of broomtails."

Ben Barrington had been sitting quietly, stroking his reddish beard as he listened to the others. Now he spoke up. "These horses have lived in this valley for years. Couldn't you find another place for your cows?"

Preston scowled at him. "You know how dry it's been this summer. This valley's the only decent grazing place around that has a trickle of water left." He warmed his hands by the fire. "I figure it's either them or me, and whoever stands in my way is going to live to regret it. Do you catch my drift?"

Ben couldn't afford to make trouble; he had a young daughter who lived with him on Preston's ranch. He nodded and looked away.

Jake looked worried. "What concerns me is how we'll make sure we don't get caught. Being sent to jail for harassing wild horses isn't my idea of fun."

Preston waved off this idea with one hand. "If a few horses happen to fall and break a leg tomorrow, it's not our fault. And if some accidentally jump off those cliffs, who's to know? No one's ever going to see us way out here. The only way we could get caught is if one of you called the sheriff." Preston looked directly at Ben. "And if it's your conscience that's bothering you, just you remember there's too many of these wild horses anyway. Darn things ain't good for nothing but dog food." He smiled. "Mark my words, men, we'll be driving that new herd of cattle to this valley before the week's out. Now, let's get some shut-eye."

When the campfire had burned down and the cowboys grew quiet, Wildfire relaxed his guard a bit. The valley was serene beneath the starlit Wyoming sky. Yet he had his mares and foals rounded up in a circle, ready to take off if need be.

As the owls were ending their nighttime hunting, the cattlemen made their move. It was still dark when they quietly mounted their horses, their rifles at their sides.

Preston gave the signal and they charged. With a snap of his whip, he and the other men headed straight for the wild mustangs.

CHAPTER 3

At the sound of hoofbeats, Wildfire became instantly awake and alert. A shrill neigh told his band to start moving. Wildfire saw that the riders were moving quickly; he whinnied a sharper command and took a few quick nips at the mares' flanks. They could see how his ears were laid back, and how he tossed his head in anger. None challenged him.

Whinny moved to Shadow's side. As lead mare, she was out in front. The horses behind her were running as if in a wild stampede. It was all the stallion could do to try to keep them in a bunch.

They ran as the first traces of light appeared in the east, with the cowboys close at their heels. Wildfire stretched out his neck and rhythmically wove it back and forth like a cobra swaying to the charmer's music. He kept circling around his mares and foals, checking for stragglers, nipping at legs and haunches if any horse slowed down.

The wild horses ran steadily for hours, getting closer and closer to the steep, rocky cliffs. The cattlemen were always just behind them, cracking their bullwhips, driving them in the direction they wanted to go. The horses' coats were lathered with sweat now, and their heavy panting showed they needed rest and water.

The foals were weakening, and it grew increasingly more difficult for Wildfire to keep them together. One foal dropped back; it was the Appaloosa. Its mother swung around, then nudged it hard. Its legs buckled. It fell.

Back came the stallion. The cowboys were closing in. Wildfire knew the foal would never be able to keep up, and the mare would never leave it as long as it was alive. Giving a shrill cry, he reared up on his hind legs. With one clean slash of his powerful hoofs, he killed the foal.

It happened so fast. One minute the little spotted foal was alive, the next it lay dead. The foal's mother lingered over her youngster, but when Wildfire lowered his head, preparing to nip at her, she turned and caught up with the traveling band. Shadow anxiously looked over at Whinny. He'd been able to keep up—so far.

By early afternoon, even Preston's grain-fed horses were wearing out, but Preston continued to drive the band. Mile after mile they ran. Their eyes were glazed, and their flaring nostrils were caked with dirt. The dust they stirred up made them choke with want of water. Sharp stones cut their hoofs. Still they kept on climbing the steep slopes to the line of rocky cliffs. They followed trails that zig-zagged up to the mouth of a canyon, then to the edge of the cliffs. As they climbed higher and higher, their pounding hoofs loosened stones that cascaded down.

It was here that Whinny stumbled. He fell down on the ground, his trembling body heaving from the struggle.

The stallion saw Whinny go down. Shadow gave a vicious, almost human shriek, trying to get the

foal to stand up. She knew what the stallion would do if Whinny didn't get up. She pushed him with her nose. It was no use; he couldn't take another step. Whinny trembled as he saw his sire halt; the stallion's own muscles quivered with tension.

Ben Barrington felt almost sick with dread as he watched the scene. Looking at the two horses' identical fiery-red coats, both glistening in the sunlight, he had no doubt that here were father and son. His heart went out to the stallion.

But Wildfire knew his duty. The crack of Preston's whip and the cries of the terrified mares spurred the stallion to action. He whirled around and headed straight for the colt.

A scream escaped from Ben's lips. Just then, Preston's horse lost its footing. Horse and rider went down hard on their sides. The other cowboys stopped, and Wildfire turned back to look.

Preston's voice was sharp with pain. "I think my leg's broke. You fellows got to get me to a doctor quick. Goldurn, and we were so close to the end!" The rancher strained to look toward the stallion and mares a safe distance away. Wildfire tossed his head and let out a shrill neigh.

"Don't look so smug there, mister," Preston yelled. "You may not be feeding the coyotes tonight, but you will. You will." He turned his writhing face to his men. "The next time we won't play around with these cliffs. We're just going to shoot them down."

Ben waited to see if Preston would blame the accident on him. But the older man didn't seem to have heard the cry that might have startled his horse. Relieved, Ben busied himself searching for a suitable splint for the broken leg. It would be a long journey back for Preston.

The band of wild horses watched as the cowboys disappeared over the crest of a hill. Wildfire turned his attention to his mares. The sharp rocks had given many bloody hoofs. Several others had swollen joints from the long run. Starfire, the foal of the golden palomino, had a long scratch from being scraped against a rock ledge. Every horse was feeling battered and sore. But Ol' Dan was hurt the most. He lifted his left front leg. The foot dangled, broken when he had slipped on the loose stones in his haste to flee.

Knowing there was nothing he could do for Ol' Dan, Wildfire concentrated on finding water for the band. This was unfamiliar country, so the stallion had no way of knowing where the water holes might be. He found a shady spot to escape from the August heat. The foals were allowed to rest and nurse, but then Wildfire was again commanding them to follow. He found a deer trail, experience having shown him that every path in arid land must lead to water, and the horses followed it. Ol' Dan tried to keep up, hopping along on three legs. At last he stopped. They never saw him again.

They finally came to a creek bed, but it was all

dried up from the blistering heat. The horses slowly kept moving. A slight breeze came up. Wildfire thought he caught the scent of moisture. He followed it and came to a pool of water, surrounded by hard rock. The horses trotted over and drank greedily. Whinny mouthed the cool water, letting it stay on his tongue and throat before swallowing it. He drank deeply; new life and strength came to him.

After a short rest, the horses set off once again to find a suitable place to graze and rest for the night. They found a level spot with sparse patches of grass to nibble on. They rolled in the dirt, delighted to be able to shake off their itchy sweat and soothe their skin.

In the morning Wildfire had to nip at the band before they would move. He was anxious to return to the valley with its stream and grass. It was terribly hot by noon as the wild horses followed the trail leading back to the flats.

Now that they were traveling slowly, Whinny had a chance to gaze curiously at the countryside. The patterns of shadows on the gently sloping hills changed constantly as clouds moved quickly overhead. As the afternoon wore on, Whinny sensed a change in the weather. The day began to darken; enormous purplish thunderheads formed. Soon bright flashes lit the sky. Claps of thunder crashed and echoed through the hills. Then a wind came up and blew the dust in all directions. The few trees

on the slopes bent and moaned. Tumbleweeds and bits of brush spun crazily as they were swept away. The clouds burst open and the rain poured down.

Whinny had never heard such crackling, churning, and grumbling. The wind struck with fresh fury, and driving rain pelted him like fine shot. As another flash of lightning streaked across the sky and thunder crashed over his head, Whinny whirled in terror. He bolted away, fleeing from the monster that had invaded his world. Shadow tried to follow, but she immediately lost sight of him in the inky blackness.

Whinny ran blindly until his ears picked up the sound of another creature moving in the dark. The rain and wind made it difficult to detect a scent. He slowed down to listen and, as lightning lit the sky, saw the sharply pointed ears and snout of a coyote.

Whinny ran, but the coyote was close on his heels, hungry for horsemeat. Running in the storm on unfamiliar ground was too much for Whinny. He turned to face his attacker.

The coyote sprang, trying to slash at Whinny's haunches. If he could cut the colt's tendons, Whinny would no longer be able to fight.

Whinny gave a scream of terror. He met the coyote with a swift kick of his powerful hoofs, sending him spinning back. The coyote attacked again. This time Whinny felt vicious teeth tearing into his shoulder. With all the strength he had left, Whinny whirled around and lashed out at the attacker with bared teeth and cutting hoofs.

The coyote knew he was outmatched by the desperate horse. He finally stumbled away, leaving Whinny to lie exhausted in the driving rain, his body shaking from pain, terror, and the cold. Sometime in the early part of the morning, the rain let up, and the young horse slept.

But with the dawn came peace. By mid-morning, the sun was bright in a world of color. A perfect rainbow spanned the sky. Drops of water clinging to the leaves created tiny rainbows of their own. Pools of water were diamond-bright in the green hills. Birds flitted here and there, their blue and scarlet colors flashing through the sky.

But Whinny saw none of this; his shoulder hurt, and he was lost and alone. He frantically searched for his mother, but she was nowhere to be seen. At last, he continued on his way. When he came to an old streambed where the rain had collected, he lay down and rolled in the mud. It caked on his hide, stopping the flow of blood and protecting the gash.

Whinny's senses led him toward the lowlands. He traveled at a steady pace, and before nightfall he noticed a change in the terrain. In a clearing in the hills he discovered a little pocket of lushness. One patch led to another, and another.

Here was the spot where he had had the encounter with the skunk. Beyond that hill was where the antelope had hidden. He knew he was nearing home.

Starfire saw him first and came running. She sniffed at the gash in his shoulder, then licked it. Whinny could see his mother grazing off in the distance. When she spotted him, she ran over, too.

The rain had made the valley lush and beautiful. The grass was so soft and cool on his feet, the air so sweet, the picture of the contented band cropping grass so pleasant that he gave a great whinny of delight. Oh, but it was good to be home!

CHAPTER 4

The band spent the remaining summer days grazing in the meadow and relaxing in the shade. Only the insects disturbed their leisure. The horses encouraged blackbirds to sit on their necks, where they could peck away at the bugs. When the air was still and the flies unbearable, the horses would line up next to each other so they could swish one another's backs with their tails.

On these lazy afternoons Whinny would start mock fights with the honey-colored colt. They had fun bucking and rearing, kicking and squealing. After getting the best of his opponent, Whinny would turn his attention to Starfire and challenge her to a race. Around and around the valley they galloped, sending clods of dirt flying.

Soon the nights began getting chilly with the first touch of autumn. Yellow heart-shaped leaves from the cottonwood trees floated silently down the stream. Thickets of wild gooseberry and currant bushes added touches of color to the countryside.

V-shaped patterns of geese could be seen overhead. The horses were grazing continuously, snatching anything edible between their strong teeth, knowing snow would soon cover the land.

Whinny was six months old now. One day, when he tried to nurse from his mother, she turned and snapped at him. Whinny stared at her in surprise. He tried again, but got the same response. By nightfall, the ache in his stomach was painful. In desperation, he bent his head down to the grass.

In the past Whinny had eaten grass more for variety than for sustenance. Now things were different. He pulled up a small tuft of the amber-colored grass and chewed it. He took another bite, then another. This was how Whinny was weaned.

The golden days of autumn passed peacefully for Whinny and the band. As winter approached, the last of the wildflowers, goldenrod, and forget-me-nots dried up and blew away. One especially chilly morning, the horses discovered that frost had stiffened the grass and ice had formed on the edge of their stream. Soon they would have to break through to get their water, or be satisfied with eating snow. That night they moved to the sheltered southern section of the valley, their winter home.

Whinny's muscles were thickening and he was filling out. His winter coat was longer and heavier, and had changed in color to a dark reddish brown. Other animals were preparing for winter as well. The snowshoe rabbit and ermine had changed their

brown coats for white, allowing them to hide in the snow. Great herds of elk, cream-colored antelope, and mule deer could be seen migrating to lower ground, where the snow would be less deep.

One day the horses woke up to find their brown-and-gold valley completely covered with white. The snow was falling so thickly they had to paw down more than a foot to find withered grass. Whinny stared at the flakes as they fell, fascinated with the soft, wet, feathery things. He thrust his muzzle into a pile of snow to see how it tasted: disappointing.

The nights were long, and the howls of the coyotes and wolves echoed through the valley. When Whinny heard their wails, he trembled.

It snowed almost daily now, covering every blade of grass, getting deeper and deeper. One brisk day, Whinny wanted some exercise. He whickered to Starfire to see if she wanted to come along, and she accepted the invitation.

Walking in the deep snow was hard, and they finally stopped to rest. Whinny found some willow bark and chewed it. Starfire quenched her thirst by licking up some snow and letting it melt in her mouth. Suddenly they heard a harsh scream from above. The horses looked up to see a big bird soaring overhead. It started to drop down; now they could see it was a golden eagle. Its great wings, hooked beak, and sharp talons were ready for an attack.

Whinny looked for the prey and saw a snowshoe hare leaping through the deep snow, trying to reach cover. The eagle swooped down, thrusting his talons out, and seized the hare with hooked claws. The hare screamed, the last sound he would ever make. *"Kark! Kark!"* the eagle called in victory.

Whinny and Starfire quickly started for home. Whinny watched more carefully for possible danger on this return trip. Starfire walked close to Whinny and didn't scamper off as she usually did. Both were relieved when they were once again enclosed in the safety of the band.

The weather turned mild, and Whinny enjoyed the chance to find browse and patches of grass again. Then one day the horses watched as great clouds gathered. The little animals—mice, rabbits, and weasels—knew a storm was brewing and worked hard at finding food. The wind picked up, and soon the horses were in the midst of the worst blizzard in years.

Great white flakes spit out of the heavens. The earth was once again covered with heavy, wet snow. The band huddled together for warmth. Whinny and Starfire were on the leeward side of their mothers, trying to stay as dry as possible.

For three days and nights the storm continued to rage. The horses stood with their backs to the icy wind and waited. Soon they were completely covered with snow, except for their wind-whipped manes and tails. Long icicles hung from their nostrils; they couldn't smell or see. Fortunately their predators couldn't, either; the horses knew they didn't have to worry about wolves or mountain lions while the blizzard lasted.

Then, as suddenly as it had started, the blizzard stopped. The wind died down; the flakes stopped falling. The horses started to come to life again. The first thing they did was try to shake the snow off their backs.

There was one foal, the honey-colored colt, whose back was plastered with ice. He was curled up by his mother's side. The mare tried to paw the frozen ice and snow off her foal's back, but she stopped when she saw the lifeless eyes. The colt would never again frolic in the meadow, or take pleasure in the coming of spring.

Whinny would have liked to nurse from his mother, finding comfort in the heat of her body and the warmth of her milk. But he contented himself with eating snow to quench his thirst.

The herd moved to an area where the snow wasn't as deep. Shadow pawed down in the white stuff, searching for browse. She was rewarded when, at last, her muzzle found the cold grass beneath.

The other horses also dug down until they hit the limp grass. As they ate, the icy buildup of snow began to melt off their backs. The clouds moved away, and the stars appeared.

Whinny felt safe. He began to drowse, and soon he was sound asleep.

CHAPTER 5

Not long after the blizzard, the first warm spring winds blew in. The snow turned to slush and water and then ran into the stream, which once again surged with life.

One day a thin, hungry deer mouse stepped out of its burrow and thumped its front feet in excitement. It had spotted the first tender green shoots of grass.

The return of the green grass was everything. The horses lifted their heads and flared their nostrils to take in the spring scents. The smells of sagebrush from the hillsides, wildflowers from the meadow, and grass from everywhere were again on the wind.

Whinny's neck was developing an arch, and his mane and tail were lengthening. He rubbed and scratched off his winter coat, and the spring sun heightened the copper color. The fastest of the year-

lings, he was as curious and energetic as ever. He would nip at the other young horses, then dart away, trying to get them to chase him. His pestering would continue until he found someone to join his play.

A herd of antelope came to graze near the wild horses one day, grateful for a change from the patches of dead grass they'd been feeding on all winter. Whinny paused in his play to watch them. A moment later, they gave the alarm flash by raising the long white hair on their rumps. The light reflected by the hair patches fascinated Whinny.

But Wildfire hadn't needed to see the antelopes' warning signals. The stallion had already caught the scent and sound of approaching danger. He stood on the crest of a hill, his head up, ears pricked forward, tension in his whole body. He reared up in fury, then trumpeted shrilly to his band. Four riders appeared in the distance. There was no mistaking who they were.

Wildfire immediately went into action. With a shrill cry, he dashed at the band to get them moving. The mares and yearlings had bunched together, and now were in full flight. But the horse hunters weren't far behind.

Shadow took the lead while Wildfire whipped around the others to stop the panic-filled horses from breaking the protective circle. Whinny passed Starfire and her mother as he worked his way forward to catch up with Shadow. The band ran with

all their strength. Being familiar with this part of the country, they were able to stay ahead of the men. They leaped through the stream, over fallen trees, and through a ravine.

The horses ran for more than an hour. They were leaving the valley for rougher land. Sharp rocks cut at their feet. Whinny's breath came in short puffs. He didn't dare turn around to see how far away the men were. He knew they were dangerously close.

The band ran until they were dripping with sweat; white lather foamed at their mouths and on their hides. Wildfire knew they couldn't keep up this pace much longer. He started edging toward the front of the band so he could look for a way to hide or escape. He spotted a canyon off in the distance, and he led them toward the deep valley.

Wildfire drove the band through the folds of the canyon walls. They galloped around winding bends until the canyon started to grow narrow. Up ahead, a wall of rock prevented them from going farther. They were trapped.

Without a moment's hesitation, Wildfire whirled around and signaled the band to turn about-face.

The cattlemen urged their horses even faster. As the band came out of the canyon, Preston and his men were waiting with their guns.

"Boo-oom!" The sound echoed in the canyon walls. Whinny had never heard such a tremendous noise before, and he was terrified. A gray mare gave a shrill cry, then dropped to the ground, her eyes

rolled back with fear. She raised her head one last time, then lay still.

Wildfire urged the panicked horses forward. Preston and the cattlemen were right behind them. Still driving the band at full speed, the stallion led them toward a plateau. He could no longer keep the band together.

Whinny lost sight of his mother in the stampede. His lungs were filled with choking dust, his ears with the thundering of hoofs, and his eyes with blurred images. As they ran on the plateau, another shot rang out. The black yearling running alongside Whinny screamed. She had been grazed on the shoulder, but she continued to run.

There was no place to hide from the terrifying guns. Whinny's muscles were aching. He turned his head: another rifle was raised. Another great boom rang out. This time Goldie, Starfire's mother, fell to the ground.

Starfire stopped, and Whinny stopped, too. He saw a rider raise his gun again and take aim at Starfire. Whinny squealed at the filly to run. But Starfire only stared blankly at her dying mother. She would not leave her side.

Whinny waited for the sound of the shot, but the next sound he heard was a roaring coming from the sky. He looked up to see something even bigger than an eagle soaring above. There came a rush of wind as a silver helicopter landed directly in front of the cattlemen.

The band kept moving, but Whinny and Starfire stayed by Goldie. When Starfire saw that the mare had taken her last breath, she gave a high, wild whinny of pain. Her mother was dead.

Whinny was terrified of the helicopter and wanted to catch up with the band. But he stayed with Starfire. Then Whinny saw some men come out of the roaring bird. They wore hats and uniforms. The tallest of the men held a megaphone in one hand and a pistol in the other.

"Stop right there. I'm the sheriff of this county. Dismount, then throw down your guns. You are under arrest."

Preston slowly got off his horse. He eyed the men's badges, then the sheriff's pistol. At last he threw down his gun, and the other riders followed suit.

The sheriff approached Preston. "Harassing wild horses is a federal offense, Preston," he said. "You know that as well as I do."

Preston's face looked drawn, but he tried to bluster his way out. "Say, maybe we could work out a little deal here, Sheriff."

The sheriff laughed. "Want to add bribing an officer to your list of offenses? We've been waiting to get you for a long time, Preston. I wouldn't miss this opportunity for a million bucks."

"At least you can tell me who squealed on me. Ah, never mind. I think I know." Preston stared hard at Ben, then he started walking toward him, fists clenched.

The sheriff stepped in. "Now, don't get yourself in more trouble. Nobody squealed on you—we've been watching you ever since you let it get around town how you broke your leg last summer." He took out a pair of handcuffs and put them on Preston. As the deputy led the rancher off, the sheriff glanced at Ben. Ben nodded a thank-you, then turned away and mounted his horse.

Whinny watched as the helicopter with Preston inside whirled away. The other cattlemen rode off, accompanied by the sheriff. Ben lingered behind for a moment on his weary horse to look at Whinny, Starfire, and the dead mare. Then he caught up with the others and rode away.

Whinny's legs felt weak, but there was no time for rest. Starfire needed his help. He looked farther down the plateau, where the band had finally stopped and was resting—all but Wildfire. The stallion was circling the band, gathering the horses together and checking on them.

With the same snakelike movement of his head, Whinny led Starfire back to the band. She hesitated only a moment, then obeyed.

Wildfire had seen Whinny's show of leadership. He stamped his feet and snorted a warning to the ambitious colt.

As the spring days grew longer, and wildflowers

bloomed in blankets of yellow and purple, the mares started to go off by themselves. Each would return with a foal, many of them the color of Wildfire. One day Shadow went off. By evening of the following day she made her way back to the band.

Wildfire trotted to meet her. He proudly led her and her new chocolate-colored filly to meet the other horses. When Whinny saw them, he stopped chewing and ran up to nuzzle his mother.

Shadow seemed preoccupied. He nuzzled her again, needing to reassure himself that he was still her foal, but Shadow nipped him smartly on the flank. Whinny tried again, but this time he got a kick in his ribs. He walked away, jealous of the new foal.

Whinny wandered around aimlessly with Starfire the next morning. They watched as another mare came back with a new foal. Wildfire trotted up to greet this new addition.

Whinny and Starfire walked over to join the other two yearlings, both fillies, who were grazing. The four young horses were contentedly chewing when they heard the sudden noise of thundering hoofs. Whinny looked up to see Wildfire charging at them. The powerful stallion was racing straight for Starfire. She tore off, running. But Wildfire wasn't just after her. Now he was lunging at the bay filly. Soon he had all three of them in a panic, stirring up dust as they galloped off. Wildfire kept chasing and lunging at them until they crossed the stream. He made sure they kept on going.

Whinny didn't realize what was happening. He didn't know that female horses mature earlier than the males and that the fillies would soon be old enough to breed. It was time for them to search for their own herds.

He watched anxiously as Starfire fled toward the hills, her creamy mane shining white in the sunlight. He called out to her in desperation. She turned back to look at him, but Wildfire had seen her stop. He started to charge toward her, so she turned back and ran.

Whinny hung his head. He stayed in the same spot through the night, without appetite for food or water, and kept watching the hills.

When the sun started its morning ascent, he spotted a horse in the distance. Starfire hadn't gone with the others. She had come back to be with him. She whinnied to him, and he rose up in the air and trumpeted a cry.

Wildfire was immediately alerted by the call. It seemed to him that Whinny was threatening his authority; this time, the colt had gone too far. He charged after the colt and pushed against him so hard that Whinny nearly fell over.

Whinny tore off toward the hills. The stallion kept chasing him until he crossed the stream.

No longer hearing the pounding of hoofs behind

him, Whinny slowed down. He looked back. Wildfire was still watching him. Whinny knew he couldn't go back.

He paused to look at Wild Horse Valley. The grass had never looked so lush and cool, nor the stream so inviting. Whinny searched for his mother. He spent several minutes watching her.

But mixed with Whinny's longing for his mother was an even stronger feeling: the desire to have his own band of mares. Living under the open sky, protecting his mares, surviving the droughts of summer and the blizzards of winter—this was what was in store for him.

Whinny nickered a good-bye to Shadow, then whirled around and nickered an invitation to Starfire. He loped up to meet her, and together the two yearlings raced toward the beckoning hills.

PART II

CHAPTER 6

The valley gave rise to foothills dotted with the pinks of wild roses. As Whinny and Starfire traveled on through the vast Wyoming countryside, the muffled clumping of their hoofs against the patches of vegetation and sagebrush and the occasional sneezes as they blew dust from their nostrils were the only sounds they made.

They took time to watch a jackrabbit and fox play a dangerous game of hide-and-seek. Starfire was the first to see the sudden streak of white. The white-tailed rabbit exploded into full flight with a red fox two steps behind. The fox tried to cut off its quarry, but the rabbit leaped high and sailed right over the fox. Then he flattened his long ears against his neck and shoulders and bounded to the nearest patch of brush. He watched as the fox sniffed him out, getting closer and closer. At the last possible second, the jackrabbit bounded out and the contest began again.

When the horses came to the crest of a hill, they startled a band of antelope. Ten pairs of black shining eyes hedged with black eyelashes stared at them. The antelopes' beautiful tawny bodies were decorated with dark markings; the largest one sported a set of black antlers. As Whinny and Starfire watched, one of the antelope raised the white hairs on its rump. It gave off a flash of light. Soon after the warning signal was given, the area was dotted with flying white rump patches. Starfire sniffed the air, then sneezed. The antelope had left behind their strong, musky scent.

There was so much to see and learn about in the hills. Whinny and Starfire came across a sage-grouse courting arena. The ground had been trampled bare by the strutting of several dozen cocks. As the horses watched, a hen walked toward the center of the arena. All around her stood young cocks with pointed tail feathers spread wide and chests puffed out to reveal their inflated neck sacs. Some of the cocks began to strut while others danced. One of the birds contracted his neck muscles, and the resounding plopping noise was so loud Starfire bolted in fear. Whinny nickered to her, and she came back slowly. Together they continued to travel over the hills.

When a pair of red-tailed hawks went soaring by, Starfire started to follow them, curious to see what they would do. Whinny went galloping after her.

The horses watched as the birds of prey wheeled effortlessly on their wide wings. Then one dove down and seized a lizard in its hooked talons. They followed the hawks until the birds flew out of sight.

Finally the yearlings stopped to rest. The foothills had ended, and the land had turned disturbingly barren. The horses were thirsty, and they searched for a stream. There was none in sight. Whinny and Starfire sniffed the air but couldn't detect any water. They picked up their pace, beginning to panic, but their search was in vain.

As the sun set, their world changed from tans and browns to hues of violet and gray. Whinny and Starfire stood alone out in the open. Soon the sounds of the night animals were upon them. Starfire snorted in alarm when she heard the *whish* of a great horned owl flying above her. Whinny was perplexed by the sound of padding hoofs until he saw the silhouettes of antelope looking for browse.

The steady rhythm of the crickets rubbing their wings together finally lulled the horses to sleep. After only an hour, Whinny and Starfire were awakened by the high-pitched, eerie call of a coyote. It started as a low bark, then became a long, drawnout wail that seemed to rise up to the heavens. Soon several others joined the chorus. The horses huddled close together until morning came.

Facing the rising sun, Whinny and Starfire set off. They could see nothing but desert for miles in every direction. Hoping they would once again find lush countryside, they continued trotting along, puffs of dust rising behind them.

By midafternoon the terrain hadn't changed. The horses were very thirsty. Whinny sniffed the air constantly, hoping to detect the scent of water. His nostrils were dry and cracking. Starfire had slowed down, and her tongue was hanging out.

The yearlings traveled shoulder to shoulder, occasionally whinnying to each other for encouragement. All around them was nothing but parched land and sagebrush. Now hunger set in as well as thirst. Starfire tried a patch of sagebrush, but the bitter, strong-smelling sage only made her thirstier.

When they discovered a worn deer trail, they followed it, hoping it would lead to water. Finally they came to a water hole, but it was bone dry. Whinny frantically dug down but only succeeded in stirring up more dust.

The harsh sun seemed to be sucking the life out of the horses. If they didn't find water soon, they were certain to perish. Whinny glanced anxiously at Starfire. Her glassy eyes and bleeding nostrils showed she couldn't keep up much longer. He pushed his friend with his muzzle to urge her on. They continued to travel with their backs to the setting sun, still following trails made by other animals.

By late afternoon, Whinny noticed a change in the land; the vegetation was getting greener. He could smell water. He whinnied encouragement to Starfire, then broke into a tottering trot. At last he saw it: flowing out of the ground was clear, pure, thirst-quenching water.

Whinny nickered to Starfire. She tried to trot but stumbled and fell. Bit by bit, she raised herself up. Whinny whickered shrilly to her. Starfire slowly started walking toward him. Her eyes were glazed from heat and fatigue; all she could make out was Whinny's blurry form. She concentrated on getting to it.

Finally she felt moisture on her feet. She looked down to where the underground spring made the area moist. When she saw the water she put half of her face into it. It wasn't very cold, but the wetness revived her, and she started to suck it up, blowing and snorting as she enjoyed its goodness.

After seeing that Starfire would be all right, Whinny lowered his head to the spring. He drank the precious water, letting it cool his mouth before swallowing it. At that moment, life was very good.

Whinny and Starfire rested that evening by the freshwater spring and the nearby patches of browse, replenishing their bodies with the pure water and nourishing grass. They slept side by side.

In the morning, Starfire had recovered enough of her playfulness to challenge Whinny to a game of tag. She butted him, then ran away. Starfire was quick, and it took all of Whinny's strength and agility to catch up to her. After finishing their game, they stood facing each other and began licking or gently biting each other in the places where they couldn't scratch themselves. They spent the rest of the day drinking and grazing contentedly.

The following morning Whinny and Starfire walked along the sandy plains until they discovered something curious: an area filled with little mounds of sand. As they came closer they could see a groundhoglike creature standing guard outside his burrow. They had discovered a prairie-dog town.

Upon seeing the horses, the guard gave a shrill cry. Immediately fifteen other faces stared out of their holes at the intruders. The guard finished giving his alarm, then dropped to all fours. With a flick of his short tail, he dove into his burrow. The others followed his example.

Fearing she had seen the last of the creatures, Starfire came closer to investigate. She lowered her head to peer in one of the holes just as a curious prairie dog decided to peer out. Both animals jumped back in surprise.

After spending several weeks at the water hole, the horses grew restless. Their strength had returned, and being social animals, they wanted to find others of their kind. They moved on, stopping on the plain only to graze or quench their thirst. When they found a stream they followed it.

Shortly after their journey began again, the yearlings heard the thundering of hoofs. Their ears pricked forward as they eagerly searched for the source. At first they saw only a blurry object raising a cloud of dust. Then they saw him: a huge stallion was heading toward them, his knotted muscles bulging.

The stallion's black coat was covered with scars from the many bites and kicks he had received over the years. Following behind him were eight mares—red, black, brown, and creamy palomino. The foals and yearlings who completed the band were mostly black, like their sire.

Suddenly the ebony stallion screamed. Whinny and Starfire stopped in their tracks.

In the past, several lone stallions had approached Wild Horse Valley, wanting the lush valley and Wildfire's mares for themselves. But once they had seen Wildfire's strength, they had backed off. Whinny had never seen his father in battle with another stallion, and he had not expected this greeting from the other horse.

Ebony reared up and lashed out at the air. Instinctively, Whinny did the same. Then, puffing up his neck, Whinny trotted around in a circle. He was tall and long-limbed, with a graceful build. He showed off now, sensing that Ebony's mares would be impressed.

While Whinny was trotting around, tossing his thick mane in the wind, Ebony darted forward.

With neck lowered and teeth bared, he nipped Starfire toward his other mares. Whinny heard her cry of distress. With a burst of speed and a squeal of rage, he tore after Ebony. Soon Whinny and the stallion were face-to-face.

Ebony was the first to attack, lunging for Whinny's neck. But Whinny, who was more agile, twisted away in time. For several minutes Whinny stayed on the defensive, twisting and circling away. But Ebony's powerful teeth and hoofs kept slashing, reaching Whinny at last. Now Whinny fought back, catching Ebony's neck with his sharp hoof. The searing pain only made Ebony angrier. With new fury, he charged.

This time Whinny moved too late, and he felt the weight of the mighty stallion come pounding down on his shoulder. He swerved, trying to get clear, but stumbled and fell to the ground. He looked up to see Ebony rearing above him, preparing to crush him. Whinny twisted to the side just as Ebony came crashing down. The impact with which he hit the ground stunned Ebony long enough for Whinny to spring to his feet and take off.

Ebony chased Whinny for several minutes until he was assured that his rival wouldn't be back. Then the black stallion raised his head and gave a great call of victory. Whinny turned back to see Starfire among the other mares. She looked frightened and anxious. He walked painfully back in the direction they had come from just moments before.

Whinny came to a stagnant pool and drank the water without tasting it. Then he began to lick and study his wounds. He had a deep cut on his side. Blood and sweat matted his coat. He found a sandy spot and achingly lowered himself to the ground, then slowly rolled over. He rested for a few minutes, taking comfort in the warmth of the sand. Then he shook himself, ridding his coat of the dirt.

The sun had long since set in the western sky. The night was filled with stars. Whinny's body was battered and sore, and he missed the warmth of Starfire's body resting beside him.

Whinny followed the black stallion's band for the entire summer, his still-healing wounds reminding him to keep a safe distance away. He spent the days grazing and resting, missing the company of his band, especially when insects tormented him. In the heat of August, when the rattlesnakes were mating, he was on the alert for the rank smell that the females left to attract their mates. The smell would send him fleeing in the opposite direction—but never too far from the black stallion and Starfire.

It was on a September day that Starfire made her move. She caught sight of Whinny and gazed at him longingly. When Ebony trotted off to a nearby hill, Starfire stole away and galloped off in Whinny's direction. Whinny whickered in delight.

Hearing his rival's voice, Ebony turned and screamed out in fury. He pursued immediately, and when he caught up to them, he nipped Starfire in the leg. Then he turned his steely eyes toward Whinny.

Whinny, knowing he was still outmatched, started to back up. He would have to fight for the filly when he had gained strength. He gave Starfire a soft whicker. Then he turned and fled.

CHAPTER 7

Whinny headed aimlessly over buttes and hills. Toward nightfall he came upon a group of antelope. He stopped and grazed alongside them to ease his loneliness.

He continued his wandering through the autumn days. When ice began to form on the streams, he found a spring hole where the current kept the water from freezing.

Soon blizzards howled down from the north. Vultures circling overhead and the tracks of wolves and mountain lions put Whinny constantly on his guard. Then one day he woke up to hear a river roaring somewhere. Spring had come back once again, and Whinny was now two years old.

He headed out on the open plain. The following day Whinny was intrigued to see a valley in the distance, and to hear the far-off sounds of horses. When he came to a high boundary fence, he jumped it eagerly.

As he rounded a hill he saw a farmhouse, a pickup truck, and a barn enclosed by a fence. Inside this space were other horses. Whinny was suspicious of all the boards and posts, and he sensed that men were nearby. But Whinny's loneliness overcame his caution. He wandered closer for a better look.

A short, stocky boy was looking out of the barn door. When he saw Whinny, he yelled, "Dad, Dad! Come see. You won't believe this."

A short man with black hair and a droopy mustache came out of the barn. His walk showed the years he had spent in the saddle. He saw the sinewy colt and let out a low whistle. "My, my, my, ain't he a beauty, Garrett!" Then he noticed that his son was coiling up a rope. "What're you aiming to do with that?" he asked.

"I'm going to catch me that outlaw."

"What do you need another horse for? You already got two, and you can't find time for them." The short man, Stan Preston, scratched his head.

"But I don't have a wild horse, and I've never had a stallion," Garrett pointed out.

"Well . . . it might be kind of fun to try to catch him," Preston admitted. "But we ain't goin' to do it with that little rope. I've got a better way, much better. I'll call the hands, and we'll have ourselves a little roundup."

Whinny was watching the other horses intently, hoping to find companionship. But when he saw the men scurrying around, he remembered the sound of booming guns. It was an unpleasant memory, so Whinny turned and fled toward a nearby butte. He had trotted up to its grassy top when he heard a terrible roar behind him.

He turned to see the short man and his son, along with several others, in the pickup. One man was driving; the rest were in the back, holding ropes. Frightened by the noise, Whinny broke into a gallop, but the truck only got louder.

In another minute the roaring machine was right alongside the galloping mustang. A lasso whizzed out of a rancher's hand and nicked Whinny on the ear.

Whinny quickened his pace, but the whoops and cries of the cowboys were still close behind. One of the men twirled his lasso, swung it wide, then let it go. The whizzing sound cut through the air. This time the lasso landed right around Whinny's neck.

The cowboy quickly looped the end over the truck's roll bar and snubbed it tight. The driver slowed down. Whinny let loose, bucking and lunging. When he stopped, another cowboy swung his lariat. Now there were two ropes tied to the roll bar. Whenever Whinny stopped bucking, the cowboys would pull more on the ropes, until they had him snubbed close to the truck.

By this time Whinny was frantic, his eyes rolling back with fear, white foam dripping from his mouth. The ropes were cutting off his wind, and he was gasping for breath. But he strained against

the evil things around his neck until his blood started to flow. He fell to the ground, trembling, trying to catch his breath.

Preston nudged his son, his thin lips drawn into a smile of satisfaction. The other men patted each other on the back and chuckled. Only one of the hands, Ben Barrington, was silent.

After giving the horse a minute to recuperate, they started the pickup truck. Whinny was forced to run alongside or have the fierce ropes bite into his neck. By the time they arrived at Bitter Creek Ranch, he was too exhausted to fight. The men put him in the corral and took off his ropes, then went inside for their supper.

The ranch's dining room was the largest room in the house. On one wall there was a huge gun case filled with everything from muzzle-loaders to high-powered pistols. Mounted heads of mule deer, elk, and antelope crowded the wall. Preston sat at the head of the table with Garrett on one side, his wife on the other. Two of the hired hands, Jake and Larry, sat next to each other. Ben Barrington sat beside his daughter, Fawn.

Fawn, who was thirteen, had reddish hair and a spattering of freckles on her nose and cheeks. Her mother used to joke that Fawn's name was very appropriate: her coloring was like the markings of a newborn deer.

It was understood on the Preston ranch that Fawn would assist Mrs. Preston with household chores.

Fawn sometimes wondered why Garrett couldn't lend a hand just as well, but she didn't complain. Tonight she had helped to serve the food: roast beef, baked potatoes, sweet corn, and green beans with chunks of bacon on top.

There was silence while everyone ate. Mrs. Preston brought an apple pie for dessert. When the men had finished their pie and refilled their coffee, Preston looked around the table and grinned.

"That little stallion put up one heck of a fight. He ought to make us a pretty penny, and if he's part of the band I think he's from, he owes me plenty. I aim to recoup my losses for a night in jail and a stiff fine, for starters."

Garrett looked puzzled. "What do you mean, Dad? You said I could keep him. He's not for sale."

"No, not yet. But I figure he'll be good rodeo stock. Did you see the way he tried to break away? I wasn't sure he'd ever give up." Preston chuckled. "Then, after having his neck yanked back, he still ran all the way here. Course he didn't have much of a choice."

Ben glanced over at his daughter; Fawn looked shocked and angry.

Preston stroked his moustache. "I could see him comin' out of a rodeo chute the same way."

Garrett tossed his long black hair from his eyes. "I don't want him put in a rodeo; I want him broke."

"But just think of all the money you could make

if he did well in the rodeo," Preston argued. "He may earn us more than what we'll get out of those prize mares we're having bred. Cowboys looking to add to their bucking string pay a lot for a good bronc."

Garrett frowned. "But Dad, I want to ride him. Just wait until the guys at school see me come galloping up on a wild stallion."

"Tell you what I'll do," Preston said. "We'll try to break him and see how he does. If he shows a lot of fight, we'll keep him for the rodeo circuit. If not, why, you can ride him into town for all I care."

"Well, all right, but any money that's made ought to be mine. Remember, I saw that horse first."

Preston looked at his son. "What are you so concerned about money for, anyway? I give you everything you need."

"I aim to get myself the best doggone dirt bike money can buy."

Preston laughed. "You're a chip off the old block."

Fawn cleared the table as fast as she could. She wanted to put off doing the dishes and run out to see the wild horse, but she knew Mrs. Preston wouldn't approve. And she didn't want to risk having the boss's wife complain to her father. He has enough worries without me adding to them, she thought.

As Fawn put her hands into the soapy water, she let herself think of the time when her father hadn't been so careworn—the time before her mother had died. They had had a little ranch outside of Rawlins, about seventy-five miles from Preston's place. In the summer the three of them would do chores together.

Her father was always whistling in those days. He whistled while he milked the cows, as he threw out bales of hay for the horses, and as he washed up for supper. He'd give his wife a kiss on the cheek, sit down at the kitchen table, and ask her how her day had gone. Then he'd tell some little story, something funny that had happened that day, and pretty soon they'd all be roaring with laughter. At night they would play horseshoes alongside the barn. Fawn had gotten to be pretty good at it, too. Her dad had called her his "little ringer."

Her father was different now. He had had to sell the ranch to pay for his wife's hospital bills. That had happened nearly three years ago, right after Fawn's mother died.

The months of looking for work without success, and finally having to work for a man whose ideas about treating animals were so different from his own, had taken their toll on Ben. Fawn still played horseshoes with her father, but gone were the joking, the laughing, and the whistling. Gone were the carefree dinners and the evening stories. Fawn missed them, but she tried to make her father believe that she was happy on Bitter Creek Ranch. She wondered if he knew how she really felt.

When the dishes were finally done, Fawn headed

outside. On one side of the barn seven quarter horse mares grazed on the spring grass and the hay that had been brought to them. On the other side was the mustang. The men were watching him out in the corral.

Fawn walked closer and drew in her breath when she caught sight of the wild horse. Though his coat was filthy from the roundup, a beautiful copper color shone through the dirt. His mane was unusually long, she saw, and was the same fiery color.

"Let's see what kind of spirit this bronc has," Preston said. "Ben, go get me that bullwhip." Fawn's father cringed visibly. He opened his mouth to speak, then closed it again.

Preston was watching him closely. "Well, come on, man. I don't have all day." As Ben walked slowly toward the barn, Preston nudged Larry and said, "I never saw such a softy."

Ben came back with the bullwhip, coiled up like a rattlesnake. He handed it to Preston, who grabbed it by the stiff leather handle. Preston raised the whip and snapped it across Whinny's neck.

Whinny squealed with rage, and blood ran down his neck. Preston raised the whip again. The terrified young horse reared back, then headed for the high fence. But as Whinny saw the extra strands of barbed wire strung on the top, he slowed down.

Fawn couldn't take any more. She ran into the barn, where her father was trying to stay busy so he wouldn't have to watch. "Fawn, what are you doing here?" he asked, startled.

"I wanted to see the colt."

"I don't want you watching this," Ben said.

"I've already watched." Tears were beginning to sting Fawn's eyes. "Dad, don't you see what Mr. Preston's doing? He's going to whip that poor thing to death. That's no way to gentle a horse."

"Preston knows it, but Garrett doesn't. My guess is Preston wants to use that horse for rodeo stock. He's just pretending to break it in front of Garrett."

"But can't you do anything?" Fawn cried.

Ben wiped his forehead. He spoke slowly. "I'd like to, Fawn, but my hands are tied. Jobs are hard to find, and Preston pays well, for all his faults. I can't afford to get on his bad side."

Fawn didn't think her father was trying hard enough. Surely he could find a job somewhere else! she thought. She looked away.

They could hear Preston bragging, "That ought to show this mustang who's boss."

Ben and Fawn stepped outside. Whinny was as far from Preston as he could get, his haunches pressed against the fence poles. He was quivering with fear. Fawn watched his brown eyes shifting from Preston to the whip, then to the hills that lay beyond. They reminded her of something. Then it struck her: they weren't unlike her father's eyes, both anxious, both trapped.

But Preston wasn't done yet. Fawn heard the crack of the bullwhip again. This time the cutting end caught the horse on his shoulder. Whinny snorted with fear and anger and ran around the fence. Preston positioned himself in the middle of the corral, where he could strike Whinny from any angle.

Fawn was sure the mustang's body couldn't take much more; even worse than the physical beating was the breaking of his spirit. Then she saw a new expression in those eyes: hate. That might save him yet, she thought.

CHAPTER 8

Fawn had grown up with the smell of warm horses, oats, and hay. She smelled it as she walked out to the barn with her father the next day, and it made her feel good.

She was helping her father water the horses when Preston appeared and started giving orders. Fawn's good feeling disappeared, and she felt a tightening in her stomach.

"We're going to see if that broomtail learned anything yesterday," Preston said to Garrett. "Ben, get the tack ready. Larry, open the corral gate. Jake, come here and help me."

Fawn watched as, together, the three cowboys and Preston hazed Whinny into a narrow chute. His hide was streaked with dried blood from yesterday's brutal treatment.

The gate shut with a bang, and Ben brought out a blanket and saddle. Preston grinned. "Now we're really going to see what this horse is made of."

Before Whinny knew what to expect, Preston had the saddle cinched and ready. Whinny's first instinct was to buck, but an inner sense warned him to save his strength and see what was going to come next.

Suddenly Preston was on the horse's back, squeezing the bull rope with his gloved hand. The gate opened. The colt rocketed out and spiraled around, raising the dust like a tornado and leaving Preston's hat in the middle of it all.

But Preston had been a champion saddle-bronc rider in his younger days, and his earlier training came back now. As the horse arched upward, the rancher bent his knees and drew his feet back. Then, as the horse came down, Preston moved his feet forward. He kept this up until, finally, the horse stopped.

"Whoopee!" Preston cried. "Guess I showed this ol' broomtail a thing or two."

But Preston had underestimated the horse. Whinny dropped to the ground and quickly started to roll over on his back. Preston jumped off just in time to avoid being crushed.

"Why, you good-for-nothing!" Preston grabbed the whip. He drew it back and cracked it against the horse's neck, opening up a fresh wound.

Whinny reared up. His hoofs pawed the air; then he headed straight for Preston. The startled man ran for the gate. Larry opened it, then slammed it shut behind Preston.

Whinny plunged straight for the fence, throwing

all of his weight against it. There was a cracking noise, but the heavy boards didn't break. He tried again and again until he was exhausted. His body trembled and white foam dripped from his mouth.

Larry patted Preston on the back. "That was a close one, Boss. But you'd better get right back out there, or this cayuse will think he's got you beat."

Preston's face was ashen. He looked about as eager to get back on Whinny as he would have been to see the sheriff. "I'll get back on him," he said with a noticeable lack of enthusiasm, "but I'll let him wear himself down a bit first."

Fawn couldn't watch any longer. Her knees felt shaky and her breath came in short puffs. She wondered whether the mustang had been trying to attack Preston or simply to escape. Either way, the horse had been defeated.

She glanced over at Preston's son. Garrett noticed her, but he simply walked away. He rarely spoke to her, even though they had gone to school together ever since Fawn and her father had moved to Bitter Creek Ranch. They would both be in eighth grade this fall. Garrett had always gone out of his way to avoid associating with the "hired help," and he didn't even like to be seen waiting with Fawn for the school bus.

After supper, Fawn saw the men heading out to the corral once more. She hesitated, then followed them. She *had* to watch.

Larry and Preston again hazed Whinny into the

wooden chute. Preston didn't look very eager to climb back in the saddle, but when he noticed the other men watching him, he swung up.

As soon as Whinny felt Preston's weight on him, he threw his head back, trying to get rid of the rider. "Larry," Preston called, "get me that bottle." Larry ran for the shed.

Ben saw his daughter and quickly came over. "Fawn, I want you to leave right now," he said urgently.

Reluctantly, Fawn walked around the barn and was rounding the corner when she heard the horse scream in fury. She turned back and watched from the shadow of an oak tree as Larry handed a bottle to Preston.

Whinny threw his head back once more, but now Preston was ready for him. He raised his arm, then brought the bottle crashing down on Whinny's head. The bottle broke, and water streamed down the panicked horse's head. Whinny stood there, dazed and trembling. He started to sway, his knees buckling underneath him.

Preston jumped off and rubbed his hands together. "That ought to do it," he boasted. "Let's call it a night, fellows."

"You tried that stunt before, Preston?" Jake asked.

"Sure, that bottle don't hurt them none," Preston said. "They say a horse's skull is hard as rock. But it sure does the trick. That horse didn't know that was water tricklin' down his face—he thought it was his own blood. It sure did scare him; he won't be throwing his head back no more. No sirree, I cured that red devil of that for good!" Preston waited for the men to agree.

Fawn's father didn't speak. Instead, he turned and walked slowly to their cabin. Fawn didn't want to face him. She stayed hidden in the shadow of the tree, listening.

Now Larry spoke up. "Over on Thunder Valley Ranch we had a slick way to get rid of a whole band of them varmints. We'd find a dry spot, put a big trough out in the open, let it sit for a few days to get rid of our scent, then fill it with poisoned water. Course we killed a few wolves and lots of birds, too."

Jake scratched his beard and smiled. "Out on McKenzie's place we had us a different method. The boss had himself lots of dirt bikes, and a group of us would head out for the day with our rifles and our pockets full of ammo. We made short work of those horses, let me tell you."

Fawn felt more and more queasy. They don't see anything wrong, she thought. Feeling helpless, she made her way to the cabin.

As Fawn walked inside, it seemed as if every object she saw reminded her of her mother.

Mrs. Barrington had bought the flowered material for the ruffly kitchen curtains and had proudly hung them in their former house. She had also carefully chosen the comfortable tweed furniture that now filled the cabin's living room. But the focus of the room was the fieldstone fireplace and the mantle above it, covered with pictures: photographs of her mother as a teenager, riding a beloved Appaloosa named Comanche; of her parents on their wedding day, her father trying to look very proper but managing to look just plain happy instead; and a picture of her mother holding Fawn, her only child.

Fawn's father entered the living room and saw her looking at the pictures. He put his arms around her and held her tight. As much as she was in need of comfort, Fawn pulled away.

"What is it, honey?"

Fawn hesitated a minute, then words poured forth. "I just don't understand you, Dad! You're not like those other men. How can you stand by while they whip that poor horse? How can you be a part of something you believe is wrong?"

"I told you before, Fawn. I don't have much of a choice. Jobs are scarce, and if I want to keep this one I have to do what Preston says."

"Have you even tried to find another job?" she burst out.

Ben stared at the photographs on the mantle. "It's harder than you think, Fawn," he said quietly.

Fawn could see her father was troubled; his eyes looked lonely and sad. But his hopelessness frustrated her. "Wouldn't Mom have wanted us to get on with our lives?" she asked. When he didn't answer, she left the room.

She washed up, then went into her small bedroom, where she took off her boots, shirt, and jeans, and put on her nightgown. As she lay down on her bed, she tried to erase the pictures of Preston and the red mustang from her mind. But the images kept coming, and it was a long time before she fell asleep.

At breakfast the next morning Preston slapped Garrett on the back and asked, "All set to ride your new horse?"

"Sure thing," Garrett said easily.

"After the beating he took yesterday," Preston said, "he'll be gentle as a kitten today."

Fawn hurriedly finished the breakfast dishes so she could go outside and watch. When she arrived at the corral, Jake had already saddled up the colt. The horse stood quietly, but when Fawn looked in his eyes, she still saw fire. Could it be that they didn't break him? she wondered.

Garrett slipped onto Whinny's back. Whinny shot out of the chute.

The horse seemed to explode. He dropped his head and went bucking around the corral fence. Garrett sailed through the air, turning a complete somersault. A moment later he was lying on his side and screaming every cuss word he knew.

Preston, who was still stiff from his ride of the day before, hobbled over and helped his son to his feet. "You all right?" he asked. Garrett nodded.

"Sorry about that, son," Preston said. "Guess I was wrong. We got ourselves a bucking bronc, and a good one at that."

Larry agreed. "He's a fighter, that one. He'll be a world champion."

Preston turned his attention to Larry. "He's all yours, pal. I guess you got your work cut out for you, 'cause training that red devil ain't going to be easy. But unless I miss my guess, it just may be worth a bundle."

CHAPTER 9

The following day, Whinny was hazed into the narrow chute once again. Larry put on a pair of spurs, and as he slipped onto Whinny's back, he jabbed him with the sharp points. Whinny shot into the corral like a dust devil, fierce and unpredictable. He reared, arched, and twisted until he sent Larry tumbling to the ground.

But Larry was determined to turn the mustang into a bucking bronc. No matter how stiff or sore he was, he wouldn't let anyone else ride the bronc. Whinny learned how to lower his head and let fly with his hind legs. He could make arcs in the air, then slam down on rodlike legs. He didn't let his guard down and he didn't weaken. Preston watched from the sidelines and was pleased.

After two months of working with the mustang, Larry announced that the horse Preston called Red Devil was ready for his first show. On the following

Saturday, Red Devil would make his debut at the Laramie Rodeo.

Larry and Preston rose at dawn on that Saturday. Meeting Larry in the barn, Preston called out, "Did you get the hotshot?"

"Yeah, Boss." Larry held out an electric prod. "Here it is." He cautiously approached the horse and started to haze him into a long chute.

Knowing what the chute meant, Whinny changed directions. But Larry was faster; he laid the electric prod on the young horse's flank. Feeling the burst of electricity, Whinny bolted forward.

Without realizing it, he had climbed a ramp and was inside a horse trailer. Larry attached a lead rope to his halter and tied it securely to an iron bar. Whinny was terrified at being inside the small, dark box. He tried to buck, but the taut rope made that impossible. Larry bolted the door; the trailer began to move. There was no escape.

Through a small window Whinny could see the countryside streak by. The vibration of the truck and the terrible roaring sound it made added to his terror. Once, when they hit a rut, Whinny was hurled into the side of the trailer. By the time they arrived in Laramie, Whinny was covered with sweat.

The men were running late, so without so much as a drink of water or handful of feed, Whinny was led into a holding pen with twenty-five other horses. Once inside, he made a hopeful search for

Starfire. But the filly was not in the pen, so Whinny busied himself by looking for a way to escape. There was none.

Too soon Whinny was steered into a small box. From there he could see the rodeo in progress. The stands were filled with people, all of whom seemed to be yelling. As Whinny watched, a five-month-old calf came bolting out of a chute. A cowboy on horseback swung his lasso and looped it around the calf's neck. The rope was snapped back with such force that the calf was lifted to its hind legs and dragged for a split second before the animal crashed down on its back. The crowd cheered.

All of a sudden a saddle was dropped down on Whinny—he was to be next. A bucking strap that looked like a strip of shag rug with a buckle at the end was cinched up tight over both flanks. Whinny snorted with anger. Then he felt the weight of a rider on his back.

The cowboy who had drawn Red Devil's number was an old pro by the name of Hank. Preston hollered out, "You got to give him lots of spurs there, Hank." The cowboy nodded, then hung on with one hand. The gate swung open.

Whinny felt someone pull hard on the bucking strap. Then the sharp rowels of Hank's spurs jabbed him in the side. Whinny reared straight up, then landed stiff-legged. When that didn't upset the rider, he tried one of his new tricks. He stopped for a fraction of a second, becoming aware of a roaring sound in the background. People were hooting and yelling. Suddenly, when Hank was least expecting it, Whinny spun into a high-rolling twist. Hank landed in the dust. Just then a buzzer sounded. Whinny had bucked the rider before the ten-second limit. But the tight flank strap was still pinching, and Whinny kept on bucking, trying to rid himself of the painful thing. Hank was picking up his hat and dusting off his clothes.

Red Devil was ridden three more times that day and threw each of his riders before the ten-second limit. People were starting to talk about him, and Larry and Preston were very pleased—especially Preston. It was clear that Red Devil was going to make him a pile of money.

For the remainder of the summer, Red Devil was taken from one rodeo arena to another. Fawn would watch for the horse's return on each rodeo day. She could tell some of the horrors he was going through by the way his head hung, and by the look in his eyes.

CHAPTER 10

September came, bringing the end of the rodeo circuit. The Wyoming countryside put on its brilliant fall show; the goldenrod and thistles cast their yellow and purple hues on the meadows, the maples put on their red display, and the monarch and cabbage butterflies made their last colorful appearance for the year.

School began again. Fawn enjoyed her first day back at the rural two-room schoolhouse. The eight grades were divided into two groups, first through fourth in one room, fifth through eighth in another, and it was fun to be in the top grade. She got along well enough at school, and she liked the two teachers; both called on her often for help, as it was common for the older children to help the younger ones. But this year Fawn was anxious for dismissal time so she could return home to the mustang.

Fawn knew that Preston wouldn't be watching the horse very closely now that the tournament finals were done and the rodeo season had ended. She also knew it could cost her and her father plenty if she were caught being gentle with a bucking bronc, but she was determined to offer him whatever comfort she could.

That Saturday she walked into the barn and whistled a low–high–low tune. She planned on doing the same whenever she approached the mustang, so he would learn to recognize her. She put some grain in his feedbox. The horse's ears were laid back, and he was tense with nervousness. It was only as she started to walk away that he sniffed at the grain.

The next day she tried again. She whistled to him and brought a scoopful of grain. Whinny snorted and paced in his stall. He sniffed it, but then backed away. Fawn tried holding a carrot out to him. He wouldn't come close, but when she laid it in the feedbox, he walked over and ate it.

On the sixth day after Fawn began her training, Whinny was munching on a bale of hay when Fawn greeted him with her whistle. He looked up. Fawn held out a handful of grain. "Hi there, pretty one," she said soothingly. "Here's a little treat for you."

The colt whickered. Fawn took this to be a good sign and reached out her hand until the grain was almost under Whinny's nose. Just when it looked as though he were going to take it, he threw back his head and then turned away.

Fawn didn't lose patience; she couldn't blame him for mistrusting humans after all he had been through.

The next day she encouraged him to come to her for his handful of feed. She whistled to him, then said gently, "Come here, pretty one." The horse's ears pricked forward and he sniffed at her. He took one step forward, then sniffed again. When he took two more steps toward her, Fawn knew she had earned his confidence. He lowered his muzzle, then, using his lips, he lapped up the grain.

The following day, the mustang was moved into a small corral where he was isolated from the other horses. While he ate the grain from her hand, Fawn reached up and stroked his neck. The day after that she touched his muzzle, mane, and back, and she scratched his chest. When she came back from riding Dolly, the horse she was in charge of exercising, Whinny walked to the corral fence to watch her.

Larry and Preston left that night to go elk hunting in Burgess Junction; they weren't expected back for several weeks. Fawn was relieved to see them go and was determined to make the most of her free time. The responsibilities of running the ranch would fall on Jake and Ben, and Fawn knew she would see little of her dad in that time. In one way she was glad; his lack of action still puzzled and saddened her. But she found herself missing him, and without Whinny to occupy her free time, she would have been lonely.

Whinny was lonely as well. He was still kept apart from the domestic horses. The isolation he felt during the day was almost as bad as the physical pain he had felt during the rodeo season. He knew only the confines of his stall and the small corral. He spent his days in the north end of the corral, pacing up and down the fence line, staring wistfully out at the distant hills. He still hadn't forgotten Starfire, and he looked for her hour after hour. The one bright time in his day was when he heard the school bus rumbling down the road, bringing Fawn home.

The day after Larry and Preston's departure, Whinny watched hopefully as the bus came into sight. Fawn took care of Dolly, then walked slowly up to the colt.

"And how is my Red today? Imagine giving you the name of Red Devil." Fawn spoke in a gentle, soothing voice as she walked closer to the corral fence. "Well, I won't call you that." By now she was leaning against the fence posts. "Come here, I won't hurt you." She reached out and touched the end of Whinny's nose.

The horse quickly turned his head, but he didn't walk away. Fawn slid underneath the fence. She took a step closer and slowly brought her hand to his shoulder. She could feel him quivering as she stroked his glossy coat. Her father had taught her to stroke rather than pat a horse, because the motion would remind the horse of his mother's licking, soothing tongue.

"There now, it's all right. I'm your friend; don't be afraid." But all of a sudden Whinny snorted, kicked up his heels, and pranced away. He stopped when he reached the fence. Then he turned and looked at Fawn. "So, you're a bit of a tease, are you? I know how to win you over," she said softly.

Fawn went into the barn and opened a sack of oats. She scooped some up in her hand and cautiously approached the wild horse. His ears went back, then forward. He stretched out his nose, trying to get at the oats without coming too close. He sniffed at them and took one step closer. "Come on, boy. It's all right. Have some good grain," Fawn said.

Whinny needed the closeness and warmth of a fellow creature. At last he lowered his muzzle and began to munch the oats. Fawn stepped closer to him and stroked him under the chin. She smiled with pleasure.

The next day, when Whinny heard Fawn's special low-high-low whistle, he nickered to her. Fawn hugged him, and he didn't move away. She spent the afternoon grooming his coat.

At first she brushed him gently, but then, as he stood quietly, she stroked harder, making the red highlights shine. While she worked at untangling his mane and tail, she talked to him. "Maybe someday you'll let me sit on that red back of yours. How about it, Red, would you let me do that?" Whinny turned his head toward her and nuzzled her shoulder.

The following day, Fawn's training of Whinny

began in earnest. She had watched her father often enough and knew several tricks. Today she hoped to be able to put a halter on him and lead him—not the rough way Preston and Larry did, but so that he trusted her and wanted to come along.

Fawn slowly approached the colt, holding the halter in her right hand and a fistful of grain in the other. She extended the grain toward Whinny, and he bent down to eat it off her palm. After he finished, Fawn slowly raised the halter in her right hand while waving her free left hand in front of Whinny's face. Her father had told her that this would show the horse she was calm and confident.

Whinny stood very still, watching as if in a trance. Then, just as slowly, Fawn raised the halter a bit higher. She slipped it around his nose and was drawing it up to fasten it when Whinny sidestepped, tossed his head, and galloped away.

The halter lay on the ground. Whinny had fled to the far corner of the corral. Memories of the rodeo were hard to shake.

"That's okay," Fawn said to him. "I didn't expect you to get it the first time. We'll try again later."

The next day she was able to slip the halter on and fasten it. Whinny tossed his head so hard that his thick mane fell into his face, but eventually he accepted the straps and buckles.

The next step was to attach the lead rope and get him to walk alongside her. Fawn was able to fasten

the rope to the halter, but when she clucked to
Whinny and tried to lead him, he jerked with the
fierceness the rodeo had taught him. Once again he
retreated to the farthest end of the corral.

Fawn's hands stung from the rope burn she'd
received, but that wasn't what worried her. How
was she going to get the rope off before someone
saw it? Jake and Garrett had gone into town, but
they would be getting back soon. If the Prestons
learned she was trying to tame their bucking
bronco, there was no telling what would happen.

Fawn ran into the barn for some grain, then
walked slowly to where the mustang stood. "There
now, Red. Let me help you get this off. I don't want
you getting tangled up in it." He was within an
arm's length. "Here's some nice grain. Remember
how good that tastes?"

She extended her hand; Whinny sniffed it. She
cautiously picked up the end of the lead rope.
Whinny lifted his head. His eyes still showed fear.

"There now, nice and slow," Fawn said, more
to herself than the horse. With her free hand she
unbuckled the halter just as Whinny snorted and
tossed his head. In a flash he was gone, but the halter
and rope lay on the ground. As Fawn returned them
to the tack room, she could hear the roar of the
ranch pickup returning from town. Fawn felt shaky
with relief.

In the days that followed, Fawn continued
Whinny's training until he would stand quietly to

have the halter put on. Then she tried once again to attach a lead rope. Taking a few steps forward, she clucked to him, and said, "Come along, big boy." Whinny tossed his head.

Fawn gave him more slack and continued to talk to him soothingly. She took two steps forward, urging him to follow. The mustang moved . . . one step, two steps. Fawn coaxed again . . . three steps, four steps. He was following! As if it were always meant to be, the wild horse and young girl walked together side by side.

Now that Whinny trusted Fawn and would even come up to her to have his chin scratched, Fawn knew the time had come for training and breaking him. She started by showing him the bit. She inserted the fingers of her left hand into the space between the front and back teeth. The taste of her fingers made him open his mouth. Fawn slipped the bit in. He threw back his head. Fawn tried to calm him down, but he was too nervous. She took it out to try again later.

The following day Fawn coated the bit with molasses, and he took it. The next step was to see if he would take her weight. Fawn decided that rather than upset him with a saddle, which was sure to remind him of the rodeo, she would ride him bareback. She had grown up riding bareback and found it as easy as riding with a saddle. Fawn filled two feed sacks half-full of grain, tied them together, then laid them over his back, all the while speaking softly to him. At first he was skittish, but Fawn was patient and finally he stood still. Then she took off the feed sacks and leaned her body against his side, all the while petting him and comforting him with her voice. When he accepted this, she led him to the fence and stepped on the bottom rung so she could lean across his back. Then she put her full weight on him by lying across him. She praised him for standing quietly.

The next day was Saturday, and Fawn spent every free minute out in the barn with Whinny. She put the bit in again. Then she said gently, "Mr. Preston and Larry are due back any day now, and I sure would like to ride you before they show up. How about it, Red?"

As if in answer, he whinnied. Fawn led him out to the corral and alongside the fence. She grabbed a fistful of mane, stepped onto a fence rung, then lifted the other leg over. "Good boy," she said as she got into a comfortable position. Whinny hopped around a little, but Fawn pulled pack on the bit and he stopped.

Fawn squeezed the horse with her legs, and he started moving forward. As she spoke words of encouragement to him, he walked all the way around the fence.

She spent the afternoon teaching him that a pull on the right rein meant turn right, a pull on the left meant turn left, and a pull on both meant to stop. He was still calm at the end of the session, so Fawn eased him into a trot. As they trotted around the rail, the wind whipping at their faces, Fawn smiled, then laughed aloud.

Eventually Fawn pulled Whinny back to a stop and slid off. Her eyes sparkling, she gave him a hug and said, "Oh, Red, that was wonderful." After she had slowly walked him around to cool him down, she took him in the barn to brush him.

But their pleasure was short-lived. The following day Preston returned. And soon after that, the cold weather arrived. Fawn was still able to sneak out and ride the colt on occasion, but school and the weather made it difficult.

She continued teaching him whenever she could, praising him when he turned the right way. He also learned to react to the tension of her legs. When he felt her squeeze hard with both legs, he trotted. When she put pressure on one side only, he broke into a canter. Horse and girl rode as one, and it seemed to Fawn as if the mustang knew instinctively where she wanted to go. Every ride held some of the magic of that first one.

Whinny's coat grew thicker in preparation for the cold months. The mice that scurried around the corral busily gathered the last of the seeds and added them to their hidden stores in the barn. The striped chipmunks carried nuts and dried fruits into their burrows. A roly-poly woodchuck who lived beyond the hillside stuffed himself with clover and grass, preparing for hibernation.

Soon cold winds moaned over the open range, bringing snow with them. Sometimes the flakes fell so thickly it was impossible for Fawn to see past the barn. It snowed for days on end, covering the grass with a blanket of white. The trees bent under the weight of the snow, and still it fell.

Fawn helped Whinny pass the long, cold winter, as he helped her. They had stolen visits in the barn and corral when no one else was around. Whinny watched for her and whinnied with delight when he saw her. Fawn would speak softly to the horse and groom him. Whinny had been fed extra grain to build him up for the next rodeo, and he had become a strong and muscular three-year-old.

The first break in the cold weather came on a Saturday. Fawn refused an offer to go into town with the others that afternoon. When they had gone off, she went out to the stable and put Whinny's bridle on, then led him out to the corral. She hung onto his mane and leapt on his back. When she nudged Whinny in the side, he broke into a canter. They flew around the corral, Fawn taking the wind in her face.

It began to get dark. Fawn couldn't help wishing she could ride the mustang on the open range, but she worried that he would run away with her. All that separated him from freedom was a four-foot-high fence at the end of Preston's property. If he jumped the fence and headed for the open range, what would happen to her? Fawn looked out toward

the beckoning hills. Impulsively, she decided to take the chance.

She opened the corral gate, then climbed back on the horse and led him out. Fawn was as familiar with this country as she was with the shelves of tack in the barn. She knew every creek, every boulder, and even many of the badger and woodchuck holes.

Once outside, Whinny began to act skittish, not knowing what to make of the open gate. He took off at an unsure trot. Then, seeing the hills beyond, he was unstoppable.

He galloped off. Fawn's throat suddenly felt dry. She leaned forward, the wind bringing tears to her eyes, and gave herself over to being a part of her horse, feeling his strength, his muscles. When they came to the fence, Whinny hesitated, then slowed down. The girl he had grown to love was on his back, and at her signal he obeyed and turned back to the ranch.

If Fawn had known what tomorrow was to bring Whinny, she would have let him keep going.

CHAPTER 11

While bringing in the potatoes for supper that night, Fawn overheard Preston talking in his high-pitched voice. "What do you mean, you're tired of that bronc? He's made you a lot of money!"

"My guess is he's made you a lot more," she heard Garrett reply. "And I figure he can make me even more if I sell him."

"Maybe you got something there. He does take a lot of time. I'll ask around and see how much I can get for him."

Fawn's heart raced. Red was to be sold to a stranger—someone only interested in how much he could earn on the rodeo circuit.

At dinnertime, she studied her father. He seemed so tired. He couldn't help her, Fawn decided. She ate her supper without tasting it.

After doing the dishes, she walked out to the corral. She reached out her hand and whistled a greeting. The mustang came at a trot, and Fawn noticed that he looked full-grown now. His frame had filled out and his neck had thickened.

"Hi there, pretty fellow." Fawn stroked the satiny coat and scratched him under the chin. "They're thinking about selling you. I couldn't stand to see someone hurt you again. I'd set you free this instant if it weren't for my dad." She looked into the horse's brown eyes, feeling a little better for having talked to him. Then she sighed and said, "Well, maybe Preston won't be able to find a buyer who will pay his price. I guess that's the best I can hope for."

But Preston had his buyer by the following afternoon. He announced it at dinner.

"Well, Garrett, we got our price: ten thousand bucks," he boasted. "Tom Fischer says he's had his eye on Red Devil since the tournament finals. If I'd known that, I would've tried to get more. Can you believe it? Paying ten thousand dollars for a broom-tail. He aims to use him for his bucking string. Tom'll be by in the morning to pick him up."

Fawn felt her face get hot. Tears welled up in her eyes. She got up from the table and ran to the corral. Once safe from everyone's stares, she bent over, sobbing.

When she finally lifted her eyes, she saw her father striding toward her.

"Fawn, honey," he said gently, "I know how you feel. I've seen how much you love Red. I didn't realize how much until I saw you riding him last night. You two were beautiful together."

Fawn's face lit with hope. "Won't you help him, Dad? I don't want him to be nothing but a rodeo bronc the rest of his life. Let's set him free. Let's just open the gate and watch him gallop away."

"Know what Preston would do to us if we did? We'd be out of here so fast we wouldn't know what hit us."

"*So what?* We could go someplace else. Why don't we leave?"

Ben stared at his daughter. He stroked his beard, then took a deep breath. "Maybe we should. I've been thinking about what you said—about how your mom would have wanted us to move on."

Fawn nodded, too breathless to speak. Her father seemed almost to be talking to himself.

"It's easy to get trapped when something bad happens," he said. "You start to feel like it just isn't worth it to help yourself out. And pretty soon, you lose hope. Do you know what I'm saying, honey?"

"I guess so," Fawn said softly. "I'm afraid that will happen to Red, too."

"I don't know what we can do about your horse. But I do know there's nobody making me stay on this ranch. I have some vacation time coming, Fawn . . . I'll use it to look for a new job."

Fawn threw her arms around her father's neck. "You can say you have an expert horse trainer who can help out, too."

Ben's eyes twinkled. "And if we save our money,

it won't be long before we can buy a small place with our own horses to train."

That reminded Fawn of the mustang. She released her father and took his hand. "What about Red, Dad?"

Father and daughter looked at the horse. The setting sun highlighted his mane to a fiery copper. "A wild creature like that ought to have a chance at freedom," Ben said. "But he isn't ours to set free, Fawn. He's worth ten thousand dollars to Preston."

"He isn't Preston's, either!" she cried hotly. "He doesn't belong to anybody, Dad—not even me."

Ben rubbed his chin slowly. "What do you think would happen if somebody left that corral gate open?" he asked. "There's still the outlying fence, I guess—that ought to hold any horse in."

Fawn dropped her father's hand, ran toward the gate, and opened it wide.

When Whinny came close to her, she gave him one last hug. "Take care of yourself, Red. Find a herd of your own." Conscious that the girl was troubled, Whinny lowered his head and nuzzled Fawn's face. Then he bounded through the gate and headed toward the plain beyond the fence on the northeast end of Bitter Creek Ranch. Fawn and Ben watched till he was out of sight.

As a light rain began to fall, they walked quietly to their cabin. "Do you think we'll ever see him again?" Fawn asked her father.

"Maybe . . . maybe not. But next time a herd of broomtails goes past, I won't be surprised if there's a spot of red leading the way."

The next morning Fawn awoke to the sound of falling rain. Then she heard loud voices and scurrying feet. She hurriedly dressed, already knowing what the cries were about, and went out to the barn.

"Confound it all, he's gone!" Preston was yelling. "And with this rain, we can't track him. Who left the dang gate open?"

Impulsively, Fawn walked up to him. "I must have, Mr. Preston."

"You! What were you doing in there?"

Fawn's voice was calm. "I went in the corral often—to pet Red, or ride him."

Preston stared at her skeptically. "Missy, I don't have time for jokes. Where's your father? Get him out of bed; we're going to look for that bronc. Talk about shutting the barn door after the horse gets out!"

Preston went on muttering. As Fawn went back to the cabin to get her father, she could hear the rancher roaring for Jake and Larry. She smiled as she pushed open the cabin door. She knew they'd never find Red.

CHAPTER 12

Whinny galloped instinctively toward the plain where he had last seen Ebony and Starfire. In the back of his memory he could picture the stallion, with his scarred coat, and the delicate filly. With a shake of his head and mane that sent drops of moisture whirling, he prepared to jump Preston's outer fence. He sailed over it with the ease of a soaring falcon.

He set a steady pace and traveled over hills and buttes until he finally came to flat ground. At the hint of morning's arrival, Whinny stopped to drink at a stream. He stretched down his long, graceful neck, drank his fill, then browsed on the new spring grass.

He slept under a grove of trees until midday. Ready to head out, he sniffed the air, trying to get his bearings. Instinct told him to head north in search of Starfire. He traveled along the stream's bank in the rain.

Whinny watched as a bull elk, followed by his herd of ten cows, traveled to higher ground for the summer. Watching the leader with his own group of cows made him more eager than ever to find Starfire. Continuing on, he came to a road and heard a roaring sound. It reminded him of the ranch pickup, and he bolted away.

That evening he met up with a herd of cattle. By this time he was thirsty, so he drank from their trough. But when he saw a rancher approaching on horseback, Whinny ran off.

As darkness descended, Whinny searched for a place to rest, and he found shelter from the rain alongside a rock ledge. The howls of a pack of coyotes interrupted his slumber, but Whinny wasn't frightened. He knew they would not attack a full-grown horse.

The rain turned to a light drizzle in the night, and the sun emerged the following morning. Whinny set out once again. He trotted over rocky terrain, his senses alert for any danger. In the early afternoon, it came: the sudden wild call of a stallion was carried on the wind.

Whinny's muscles grew tense. He could hear the sound of hoofbeats; the horses were covering the ground at a steady pace. Instinctively, Whinny gave an answering cry and set off to follow them.

By late afternoon he saw the stallion's band grazing on top of a hill. Even from a distance he could see that one of the fillies was Starfire.

Whinny and Ebony saw each other at the same time. Recognizing his old foe, Ebony reared up and pawed the air with his front hoofs. As Whinny slowed down, Starfire nickered in delight.

When she started to trot toward Whinny, Ebony gave her a sharp bite on the flank. Then he turned toward Whinny. He lowered his head, laid back his ears, and bared his teeth. Whinny neighed shrilly.

Not wasting any time, Ebony pierced the air with his own high-pitched whistle, then charged. Whinny rose to meet him. They came together quickly, both rising high on their hind legs, front legs beating each other. Ebony broke away and twisted his neck around, aiming a bite at Whinny's legs. With one well-placed snap of the jaws, the fight would be over. But Whinny quickly collapsed on his legs to avoid the powerful teeth. Ebony got his shoulder instead, tearing out a chunk of hide. Whinny wasn't through yet. The rodeo had taught him speed, endurance, and agility, and now he used his skills. In a swirl of dust, he got to his feet, then reared up to his full height. He bit his opponent, lashed out with his front hoofs, and bit again. The startled stallion fell back, but only for a moment.

Ebony bared his teeth and lunged again, but Whinny dodged away. He wheeled around and

kicked Ebony with his rear legs, catching him in the face with a fierce blow.

Ebony screamed out in pain. Whinny kept pounding, hitting him in the head, shoulder, and ribs. Ebony tried to get clear, but stumbled and fell to the ground.

Whinny reared up to crush his opponent. Ebony rolled away and regained his footing as Whinny sank his teeth into the other horse's neck. Ebony pulled free. Whinny chased him, and Ebony began to run, leaving his band to the fierce young horse.

Whinny gave a great cry of victory that rang out across the plains. One of the mares started to follow Ebony; Whinny nipped her smartly on the rump and she fell back. Then he rounded the group into a circle. Weaving his neck in the snakelike movement he had often seen his father use, Whinny moved his new band out.

The band traveled west until dusk, when the battered and sore leader finally allowed himself to rest. They crossed a river, then stopped near a ridge that sheltered them from the evening wind. A quiet tributary of the river and patches of vegetation provided nourishment.

After seeing that his band was safe and comfortable, Whinny looked over at Starfire. They rushed toward each other then, sniffing each other's scent, pressing their cheeks together, and giving soft, excited whinnies.

The band stayed by the water for two days. Whinny lay in the soft earth and let the mud soothe his wounds. He and Starfire were often together, sniffing each other or just standing side by side.

In the hours of rest, Whinny began to know his band. The lead mare, Blackie, was an old black dam. There were seven other mares and three black foals.

Every horse seemed to know its place in the band. The little foals kept close to their mothers. Blackie helped Whinny keep the band in line. Occasionally a mare wandered away, unsure of her young leader. Whinny was quick to catch up to the deserter and bring her back.

On the third day, Whinny led the band out once more. He chose to travel back in the direction of Wild Horse Valley. Blackie moved around the stragglers, bunching them up and biting them with her strong yellow teeth if they didn't obey.

Two days later, Blackie became restless and short-tempered. The time had come for her to foal.

When the mare started to leave the band to give birth in privacy, Whinny forced her to stay. He wanted the mare close by so he could protect her.

He kept vigil over her all that night, and with the coming of morning the foal was born. Whinny watched as two tiny hoofs appeared. Soon the foal's head was visible. Several minutes later the shoulders emerged and a newborn colt lay on the ground. The mare licked him clean and nickered to him.

Whinny watched as the little colt tried to stand. His mother nickered softly and nudged the foal, whose coat had begun to fluff out. He found his mother's udder and nursed contentedly.

It was two days before the band could continue their journey. Whinny wanted to find a place for them to settle; he knew more foals were on the way.

The weather became very warm. Whinny led his band over rocky terrain, where the horses found cool shade against the ledges. They traveled slowly, giving the gray colt a chance to rest and grow stronger.

At last there was a noticeable change in the terrain from lush green to sparse brown. Whinny veered to the west; when he found a stream, the band stopped and rested by it.

They followed the brook as it zigzagged through the sagebrush. The stream ended, and the sun beat down on the horses. Whinny let them spend one day by the last trickle of water, then led them on into desert.

Whinny let his instinct and memory of his earlier journey through the desert guide him. He steered the band north, then west, then north again. They traveled slowly over the cracked ground, which was covered with sagebrush and cacti. An elf owl nested in a prickly pear cactus; a rattlesnake swung his broad head from side to side, trying to pick up the heat trail of a small, tasty animal.

Whinny could see a few desert willows and smoke trees in the distance. He led his band toward them, hoping to find water. By nightfall they had come to a water hole. Blackie drank deeply, then rested, her little foal alongside her.

Whinny was able to lead the horses from water hole to water hole until they came across a stream. They followed it and grazed on green grass once again, then rested in the shade of small trees. Whinny kept driving his band forward, stopping only if the gray foal was tired.

Early one morning, as they came to the crest of a hill, Whinny stopped to test the scent. His nostrils flared wide. Starfire had also stopped and was looking around. Familiar sights and smells surrounded them. They saw a stream that wound around and around like a snake. Looking toward a grove of cottonwood trees on the opposite side of the stream, Whinny could see another band of wild horses.

Their leader was a stallion with a brilliant red coat. A chocolate-brown mare was at his side, and a tiny foal was nuzzling her.

Whinny stared at his sire. Wildfire stared back, not trusting his powerful-looking son. But Whinny had no desire for his father's band; he had a band of his own now.

Whinny led the band along the stream for three days, until they came to a ridge overlooking an area that had once been a beaver pond. Now it was a fertile meadow filled with tiny wildflowers.

In the distance were faraway ravines and secluded valleys. Canyon walls rising in the distance would provide shelter from severe weather. A freshwater stream flowed through fern-covered banks. Starfire tasted the lush grass, lifting her head every once in a while to watch the foals or Whinny.

Whinny stood looking over the valley—*his* valley. He was home at last.

Amy C. Laundrie lives in Wisconsin Dells, Wisconsin, where she rides and trains her own horse. *Whinny of the Wild Horses* is her first book.

Jean Cassels Helmer has illustrated a number of books for young readers, including *Star*, by Jo Ann Simon. She lives in New Orleans with her husband and two dogs.

*Faith's got a problem with learning to ride—
horses terrify her!*

A Summer of Horses

by Carol Fenner

For ten-year-old animal lover Faith, the thought of spending
an entire summer at Beth Holbein's horse farm is like a dream
come true. But Faith has a rather rude awakening when she
arrives at the farm and realizes that horses are much bigger,
much more powerful, and much, much scarier than she had
ever imagined. Just being near these gigantic beasts terrifies
her! And, to make matters even worse, her boy-crazy older
sister—who doesn't even like animals—proves to be a
natural-born rider. It's going to be a long, hard summer if
Faith doesn't learn to love horses—and quick!

"Likely to command a loyal following." —*Publishers Weekly*

"A good coming-of-age novel." —*Kirkus*

A BULLSEYE BOOK PUBLISHED BY ALFRED A. KNOPF, INC.